miss molly

miss molly

Why the Owl has big Ears

To AMH for allowing me the freedom to explore
MJP

For Dan and Karen, with love and thanks
SM

Text copyright © 2005 Mike J. Preble
Illustrations copyright © 2005 Shawn McCann

Published by Goulasche Press
Distributed by Itasca Books

Library of Congress Control Number: 2005931358
ISBN Number: 097714660X

First Edition 2005
Printed In Canada

Goulasche Press
1352 Ithilien
Excelsior, MN 55331

Why the Owl has big Ears

Retold by Mike J. Preble
Illustrated by Shawn McCann

Goulasche Press

Raweno sat on his old stump, rubbing bits of clay between his gnarled fingers. The setting sun headed behind the distant mountains. Raweno looked over the world. "The plants are complete," he said. "Of the animals, only two remain."

Raweno reached behind a bush and picked up a small lump of clay. "Why are you hiding?" he asked.

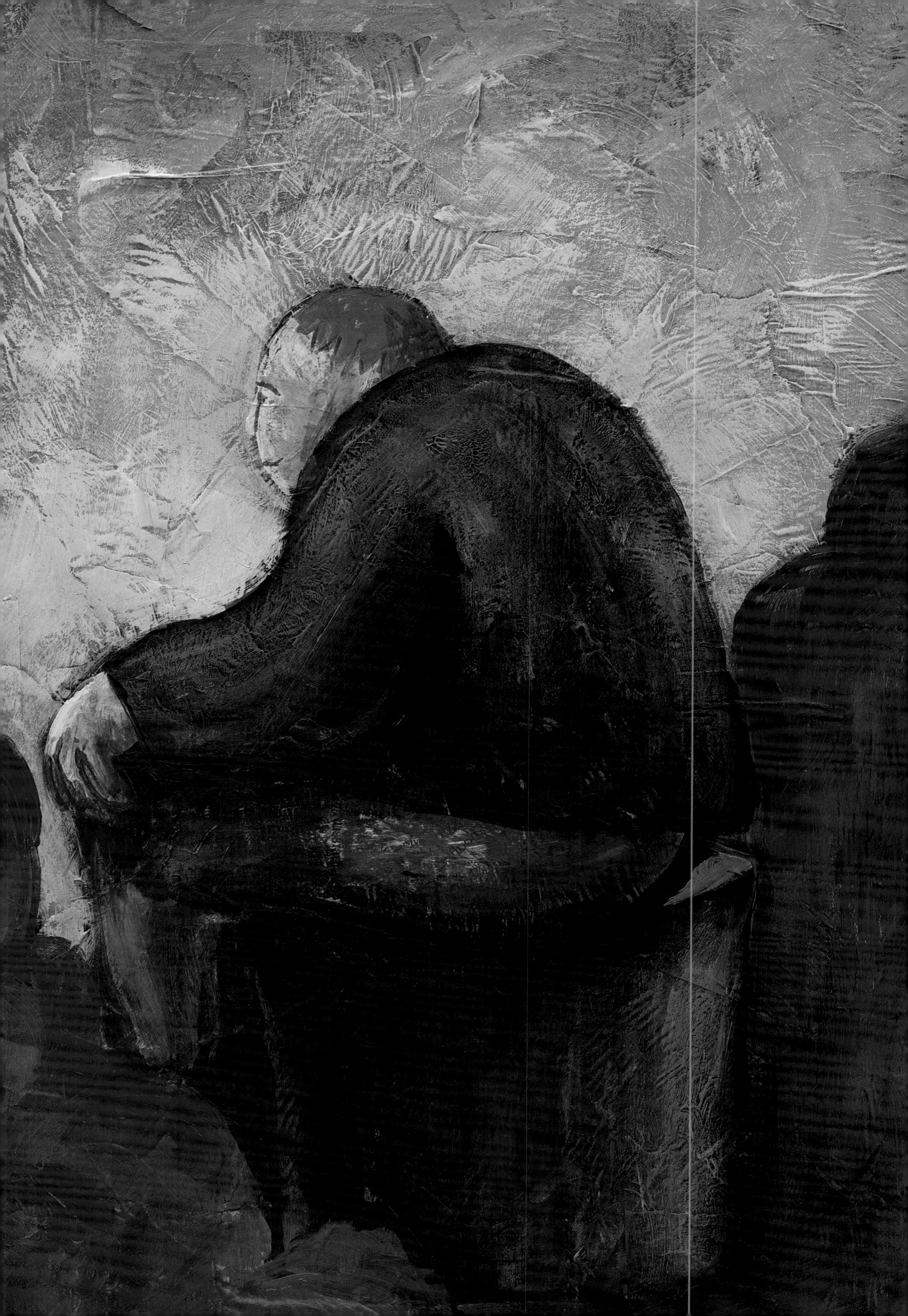

“Whoooo,” said another lump of clay sitting high in the tree.

“You,” said Raweno.

“I didn’t say anything,” said the clay in his hands.

“You are Rabbit,” said Raweno, “and Rabbit is next.”

“But I want to be called Bunny-Bunny,” said Rabbit.

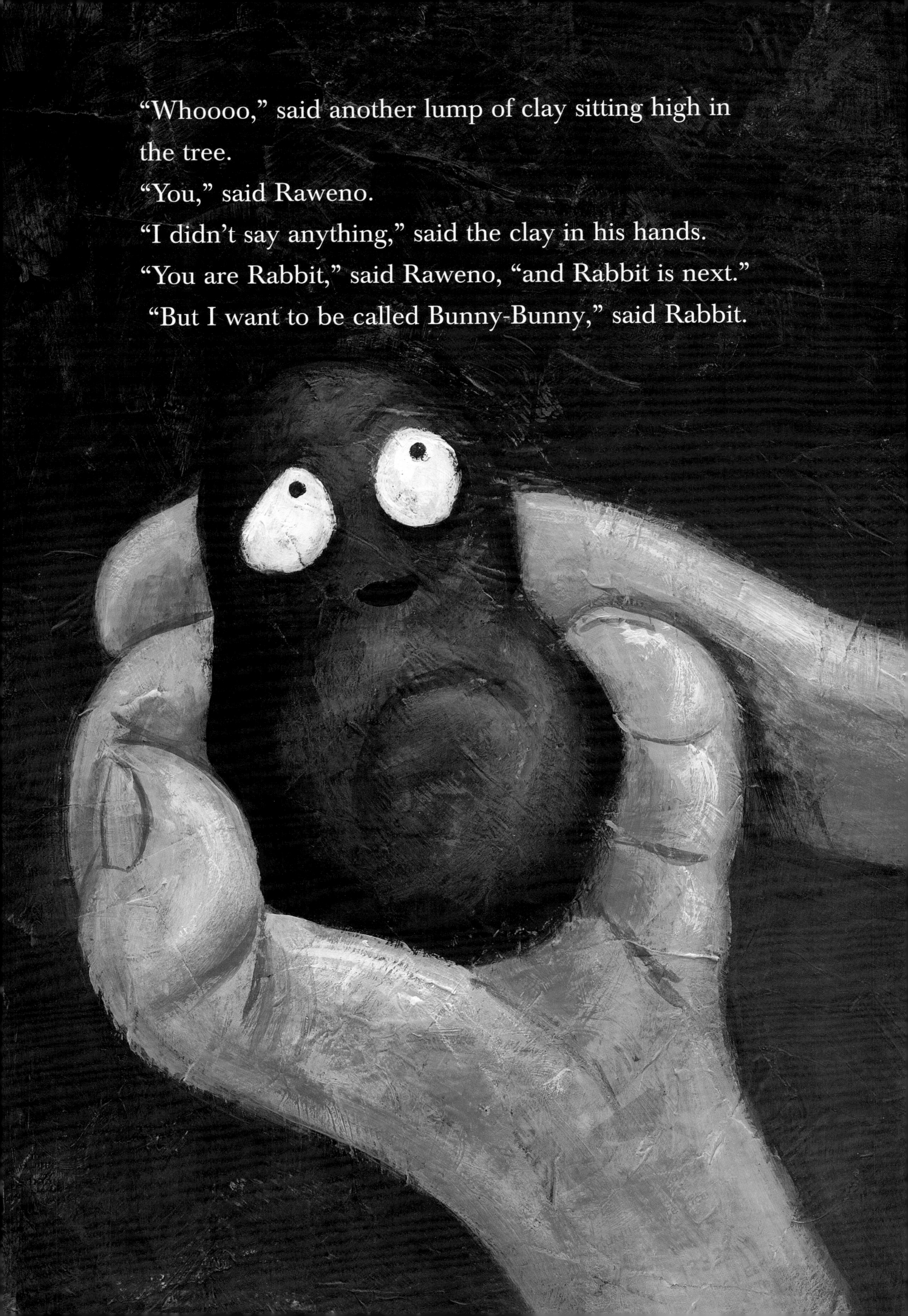

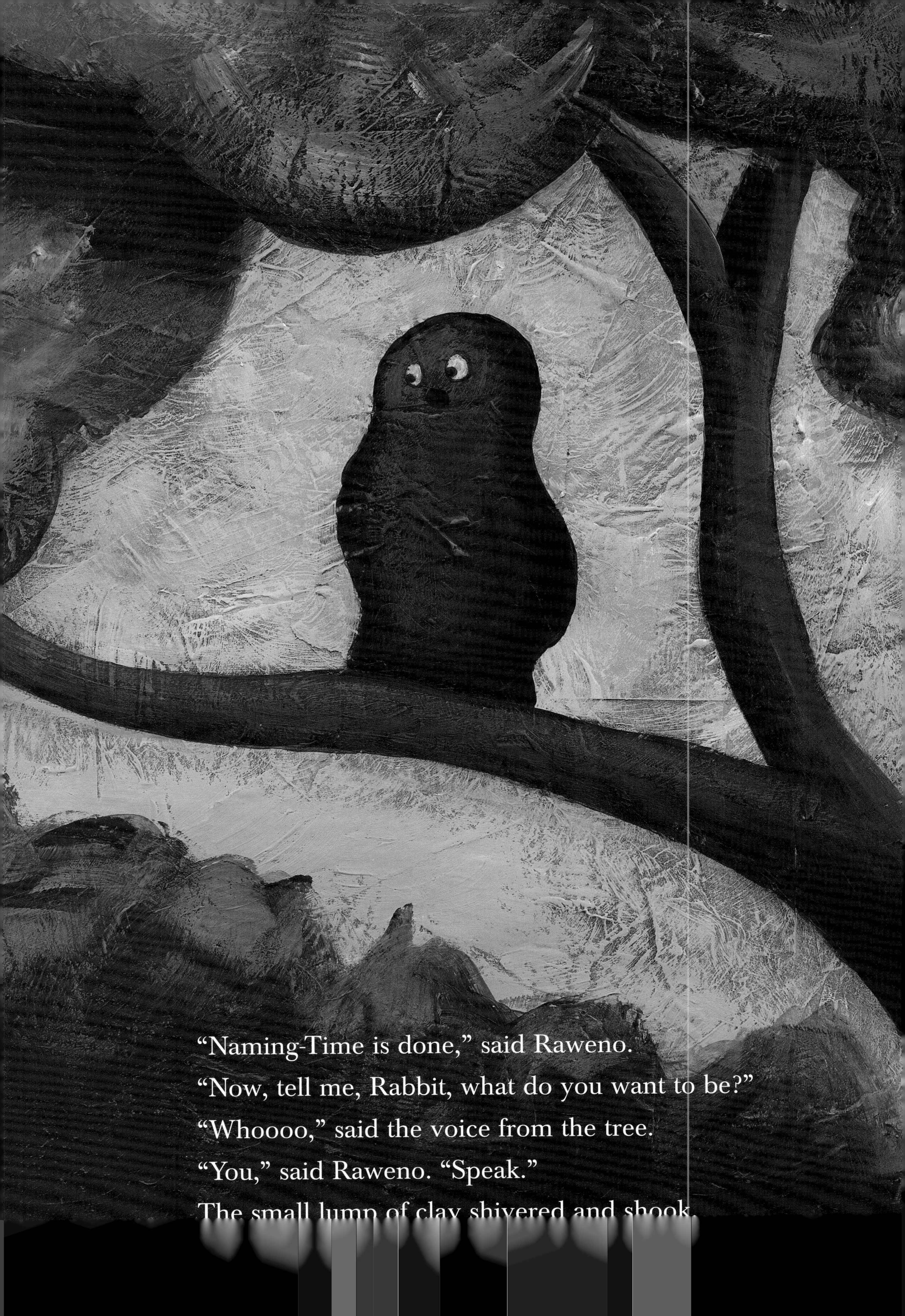

"Naming-Time is done," said Raweno.

"Now, tell me, Rabbit, what do you want to be?"

"Whoooo," said the voice from the tree.

"You," said Raweno. "Speak."

The small lump of clay shivered and shook.

"I want a beautiful beak, long and curved for picking sweet berries, and fiery feathers that flash golden in the sun," said the voice from the tree.

"A long beak?" said Raweno.

"I don't want a beak," said Rabbit.

"What about fiery feathers that flash golden in the sky?" asked Raweno.

"I don't want to fly," said Rabbit. He wiggled his nose. "I want long, long legs so I can run like the wind."

"Then long legs you shall have," said Raweno.

"Whoooo," said the voice from the tree.

"You," said Raweno.

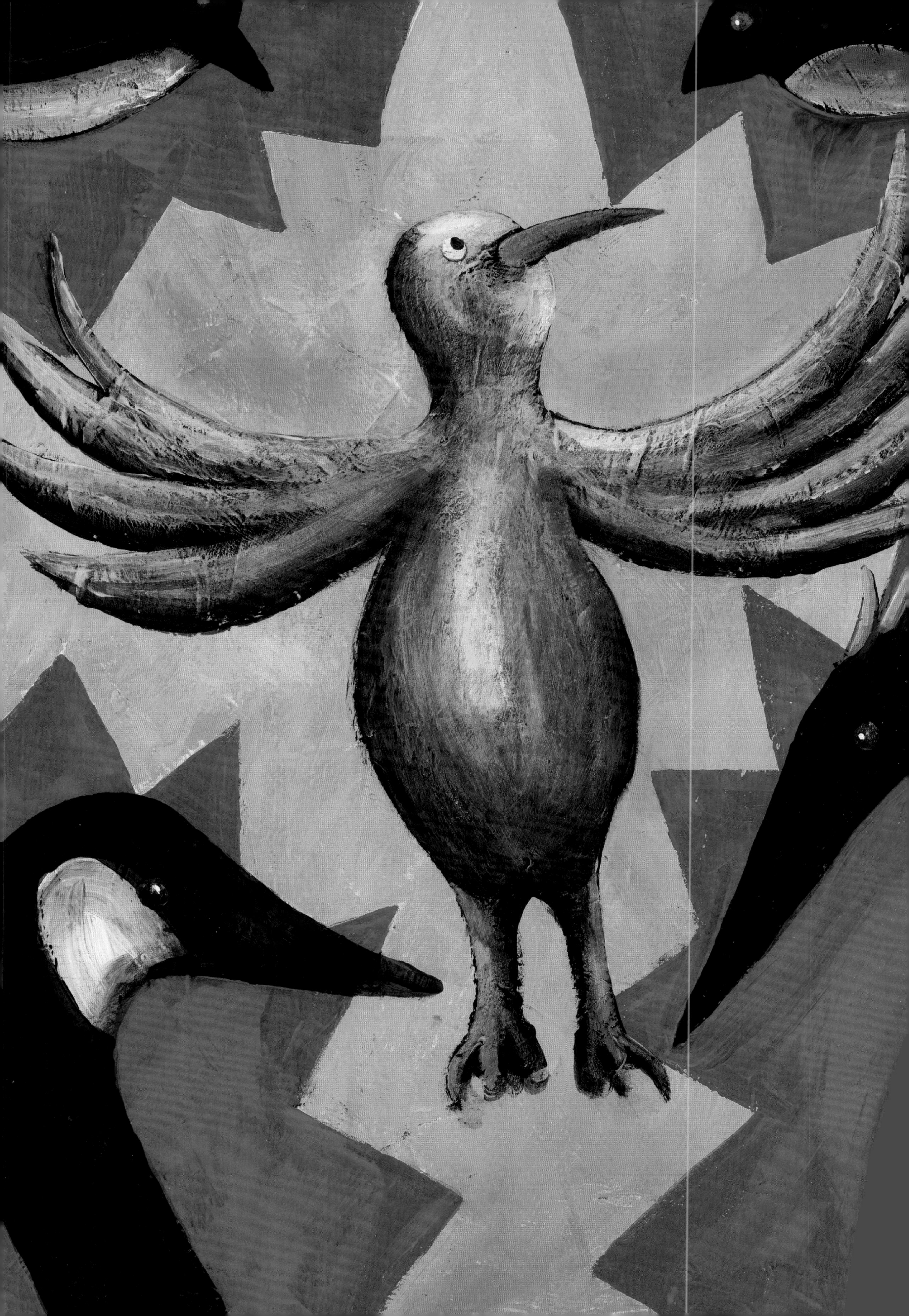

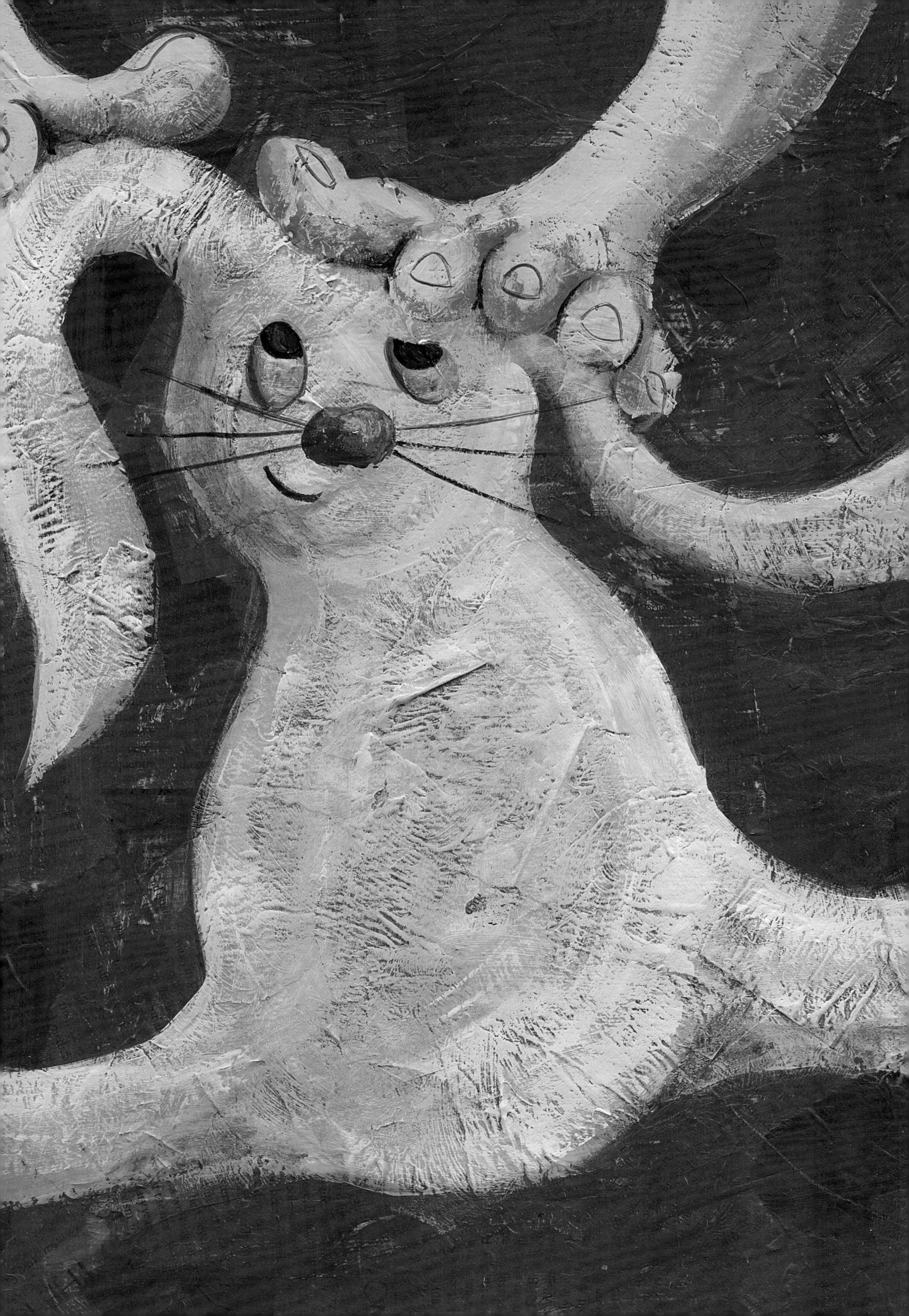

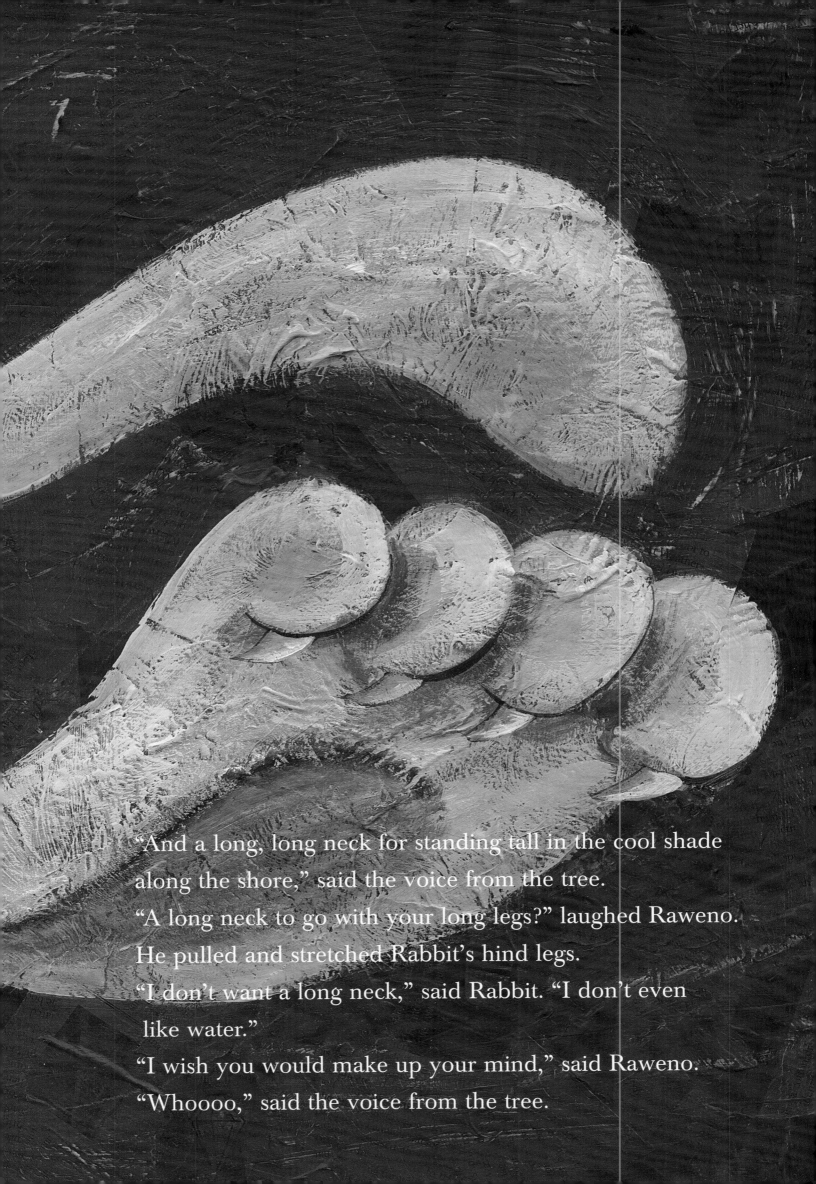

"And a long, long neck for standing tall in the cool shade
along the shore," said the voice from the tree.
"A long neck to go with your long legs?" laughed Raweno.
He pulled and stretched Rabbit's hind legs.
"I don't want a long neck," said Rabbit. "I don't even
like water."
"I wish you would make up your mind," said Raweno.
"Whoooo," said the voice from the tree.

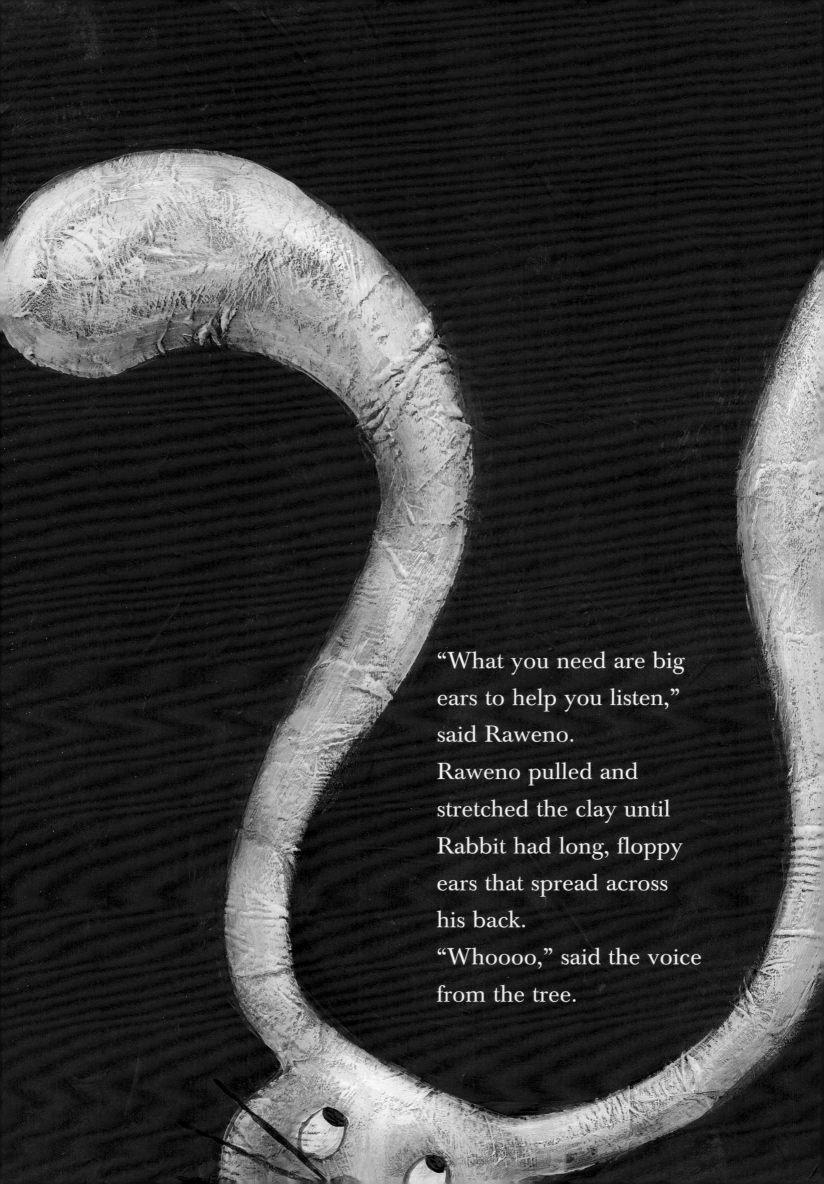

"What you need are big ears to help you listen," said Raweno.
Raweno pulled and stretched the clay until Rabbit had long, floppy ears that spread across his back.
"Whoooo," said the voice from the tree.

Raweno held Rabbit close to his face.

"You are not paying attention."

Rabbit's eyes grew large. He tucked his front legs up to his tummy. He didn't move a muscle.

"Whoooo," said the voice from the tree.

"A long, flowing tail that rides the breeze as I sail over the mountains."

"Who?" said Raweno.

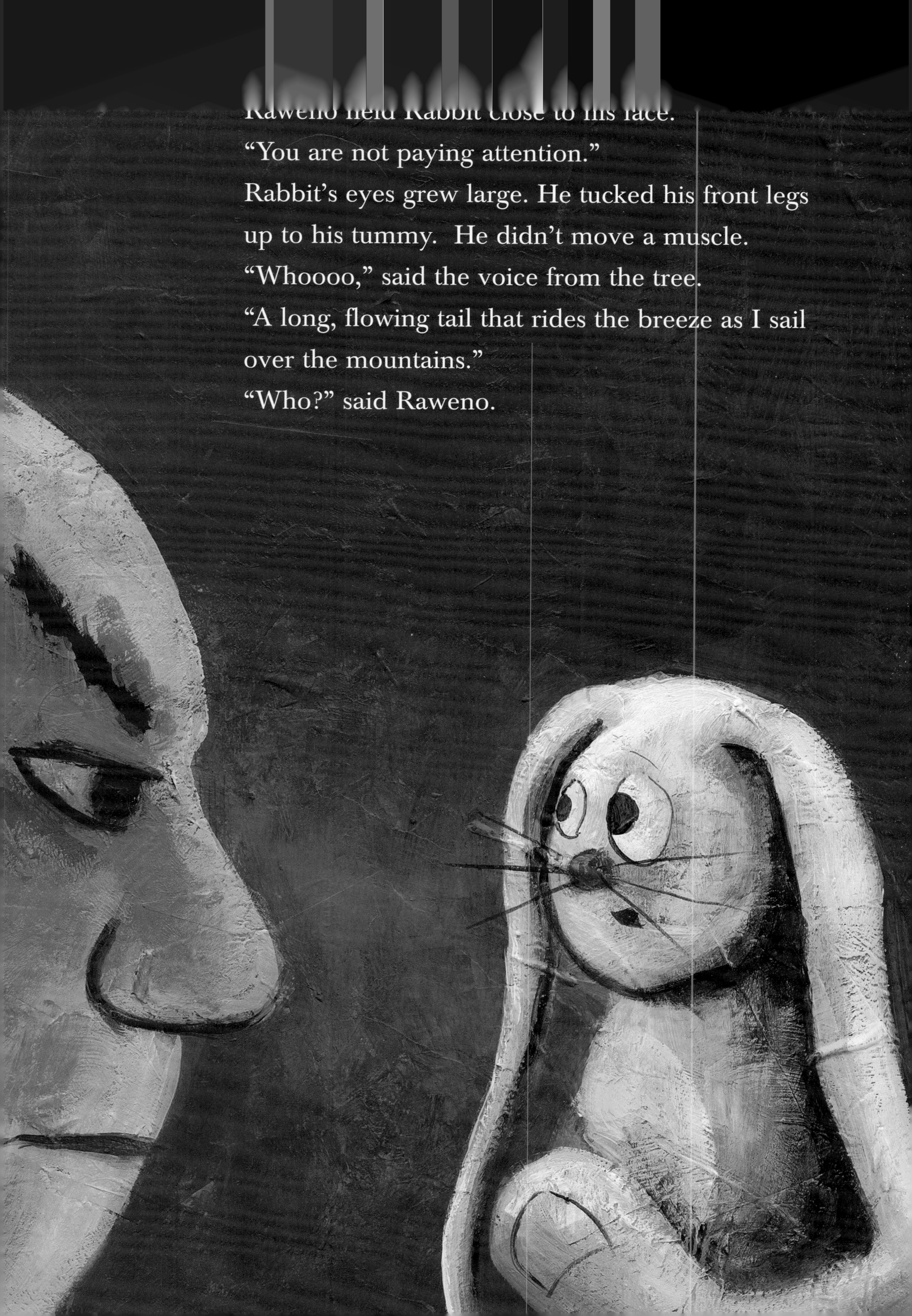

"Who?" said Raweno.

Raweno stood up. He reached high to the knot of a broken branch.

"Whoooo," said the lump of clay, now in Raweno's hands.

"You," said Raweno. "You are Owl and you must wait. I have Rabbit to finish."

"Rabbit must wait," said Owl. "The sun is setting. How can my beautiful feathers glisten in the dark?"

"Your feathers will glisten when I am finished," said Raweno.

He placed Owl back on the tree branch, facing away from his stump.

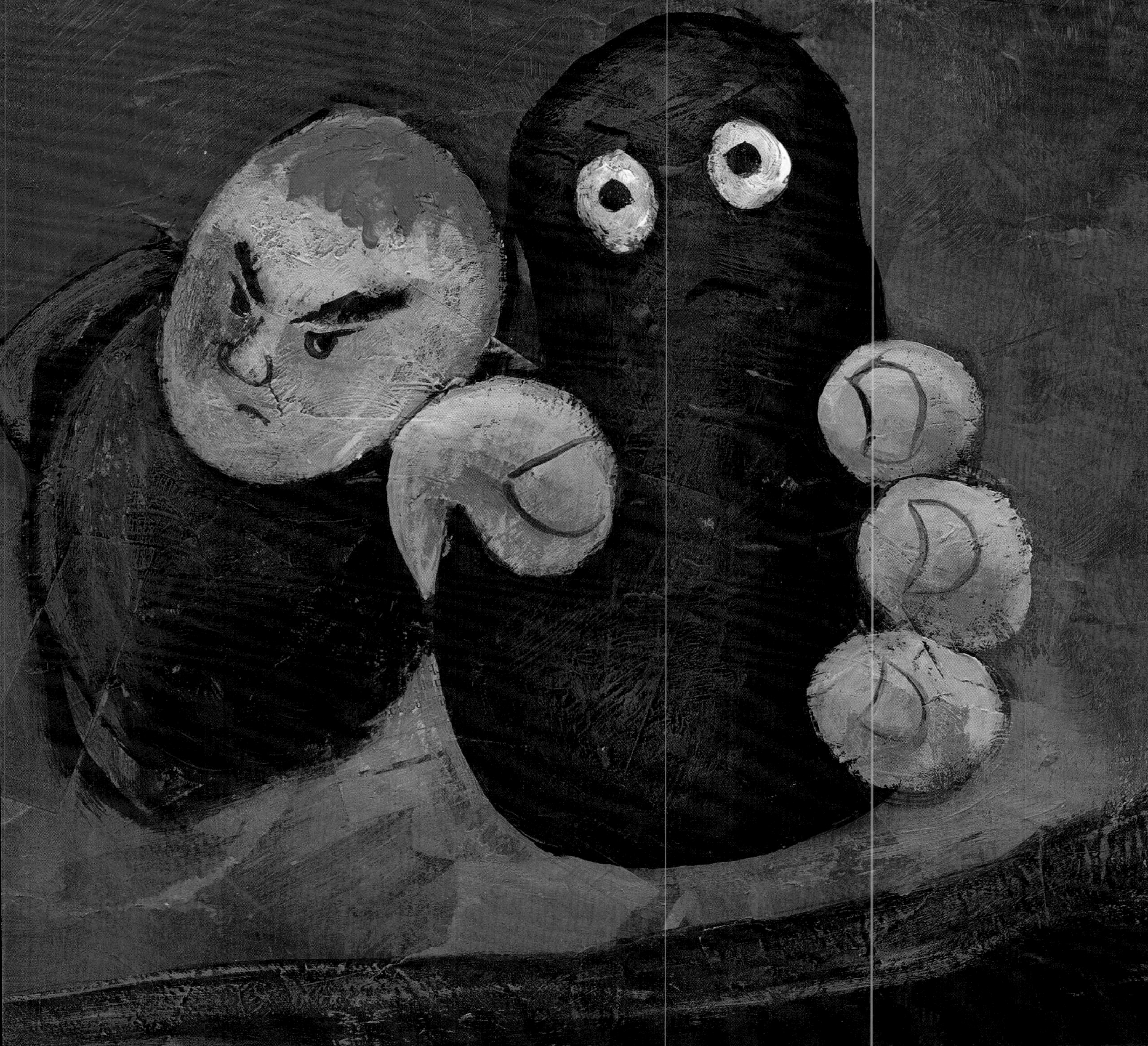

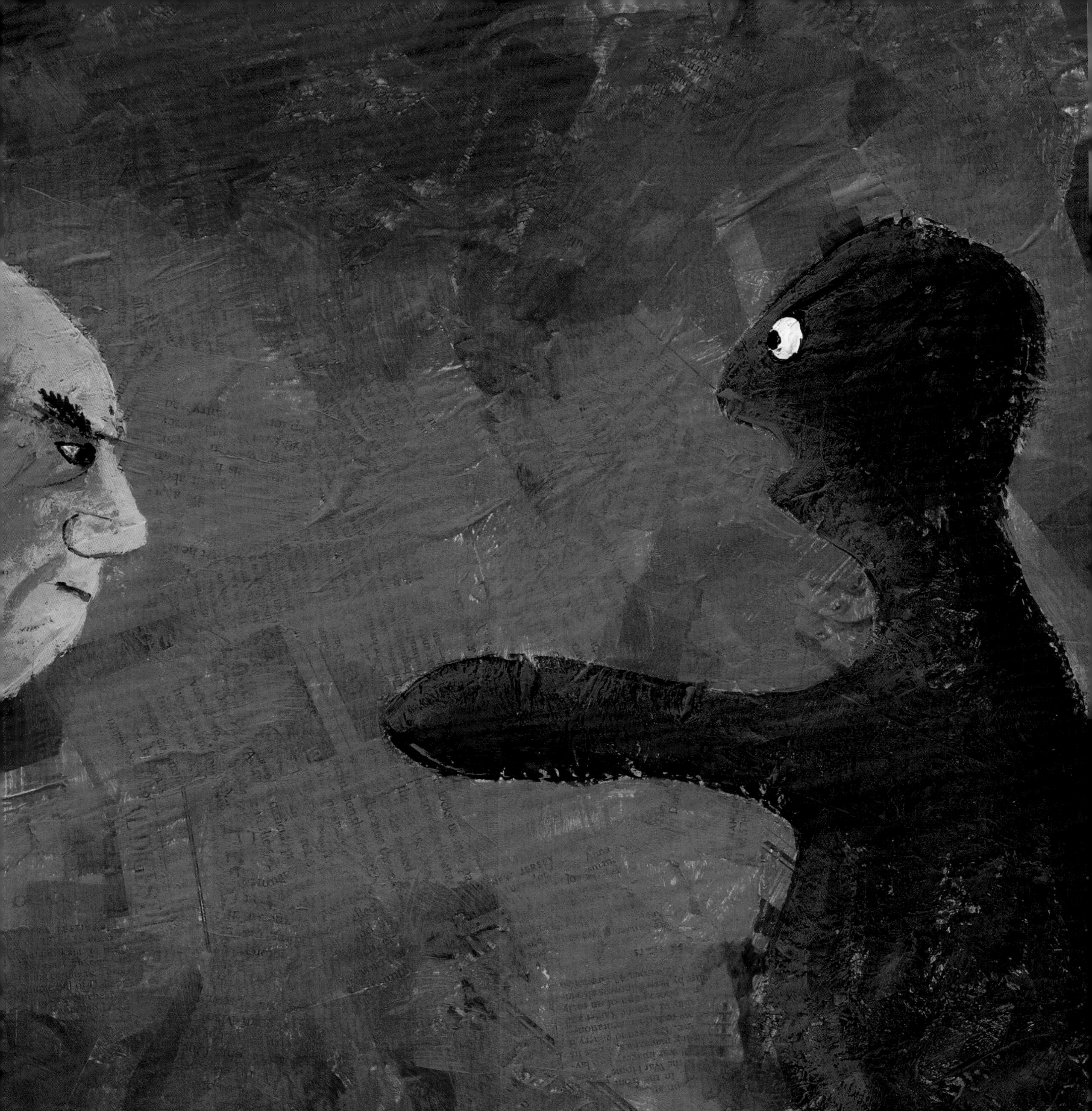

“How will I know when you are done?” asked Owl.
“No one watches my work,” said Raweno.
“Now, where have you gone?”
“Whoooo?” said Owl.
“Rabbit,” said Raweno.
“Rabbit ran away,” said Owl.
“Find him later, make me, now.”

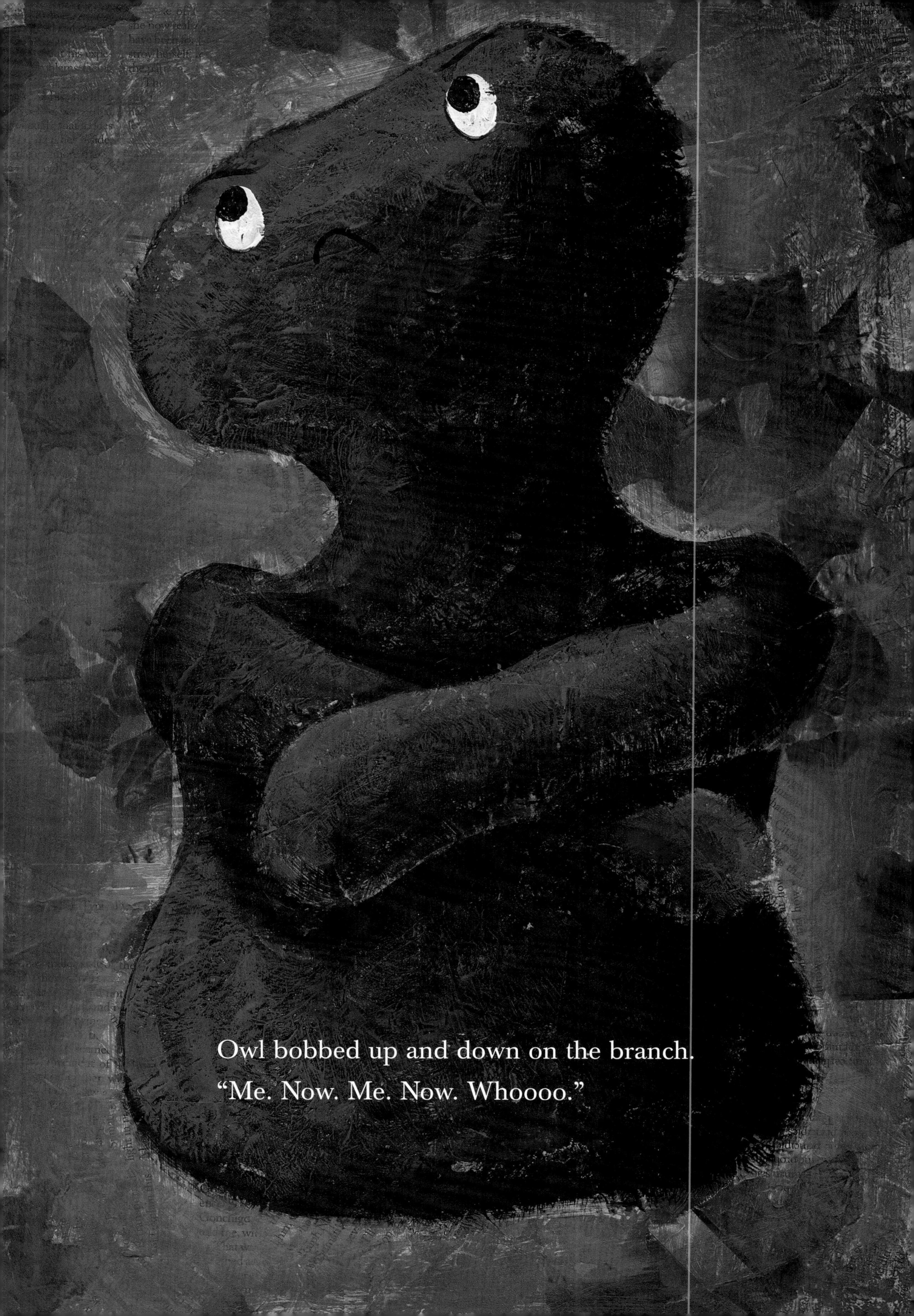

Owl bobbed up and down on the branch.
"Me. Now. Me. Now. Whoooo."

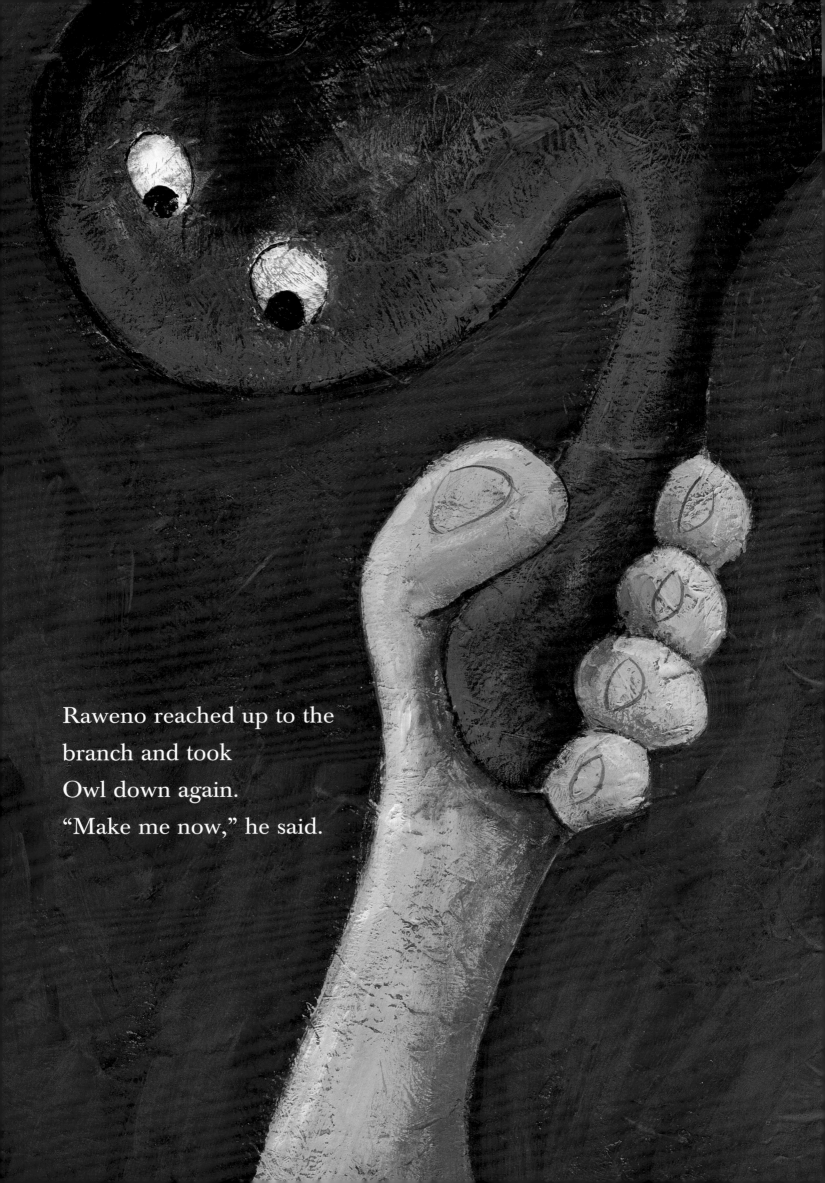

Raweno reached up to the
branch and took
Owl down again.
"Make me now," he said.

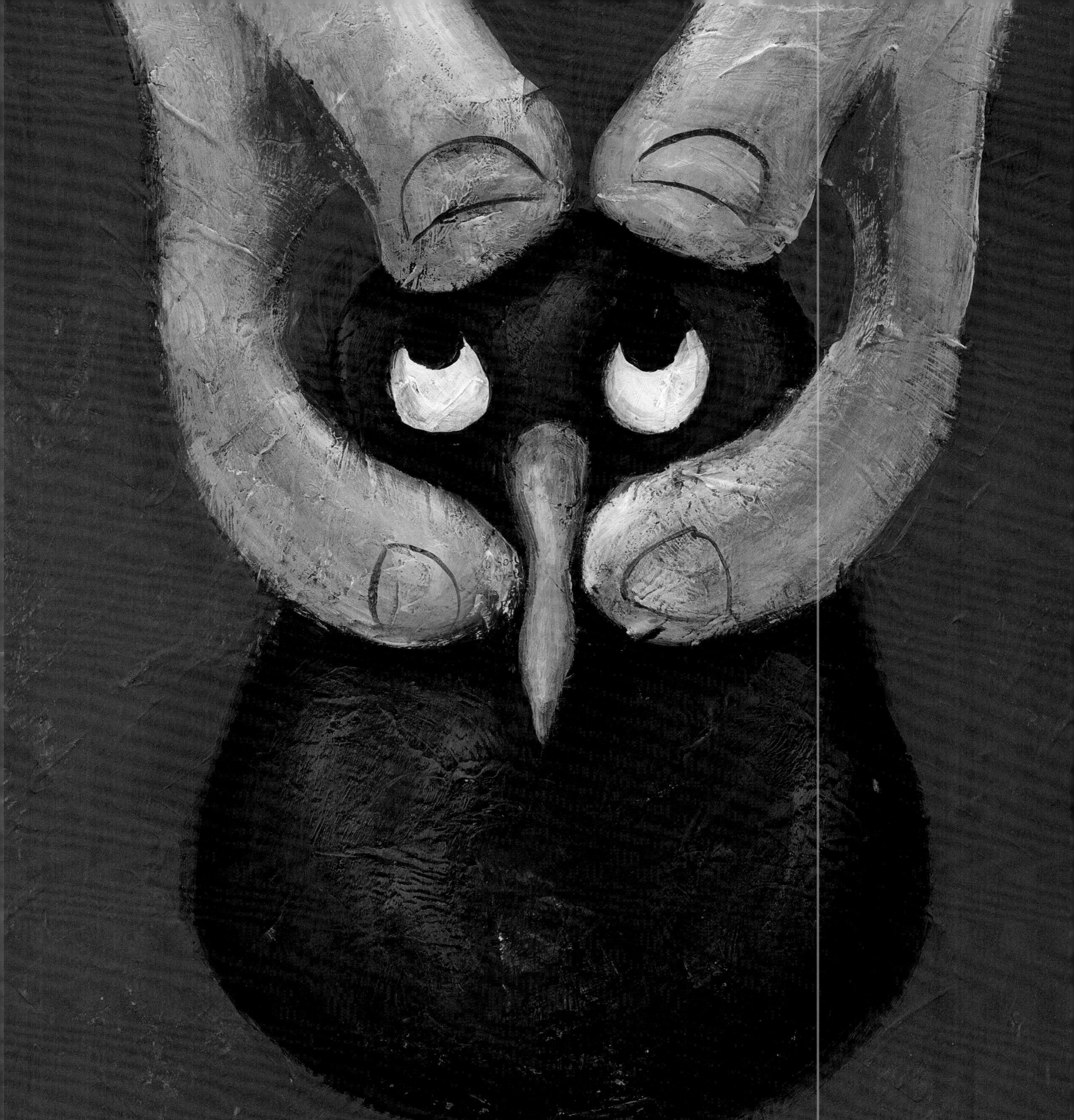

Raweno stretched and pulled the clay.
He made a gently curving beak, perfect for gathering wild fruits and berries.
"You could have had this beak."
Then Raweno squeezed the clay into a stubby hook.
"This beak is for someone who cannot wait his turn."
"Whoooo." said Owl.

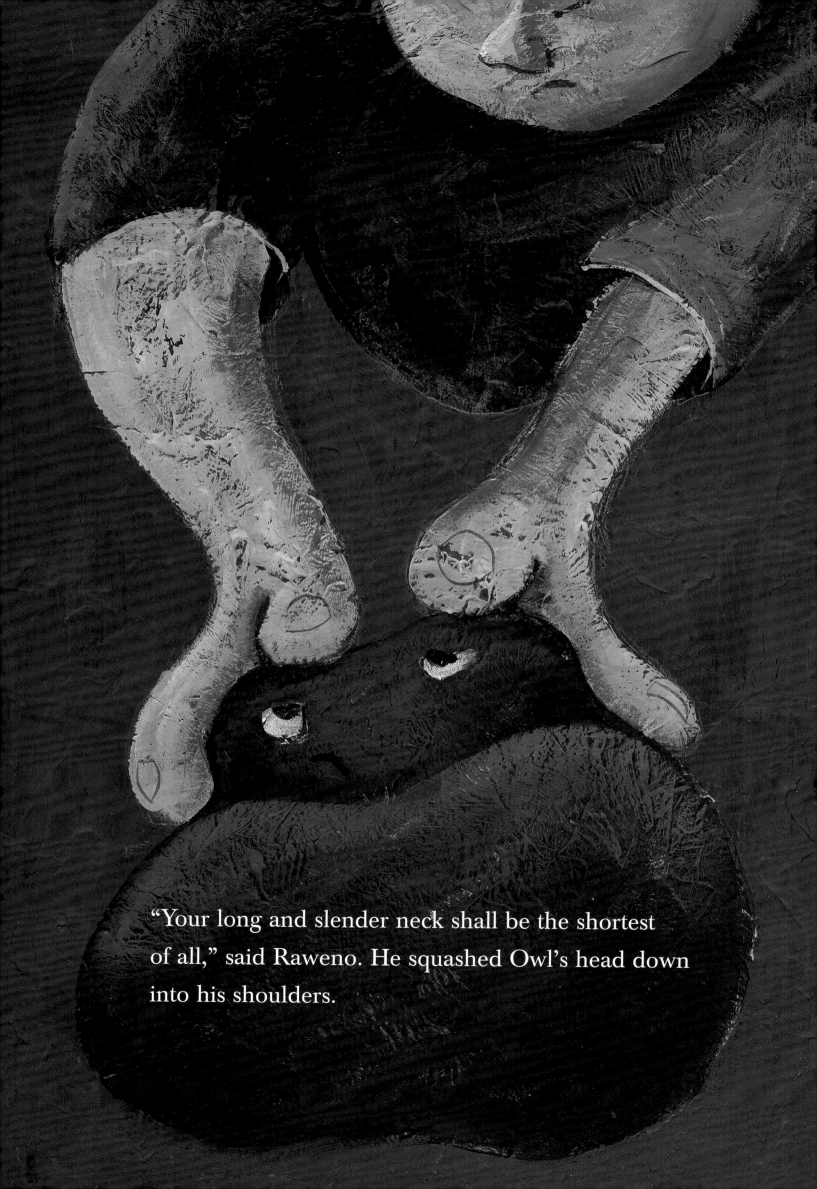

"Your long and slender neck shall be the shortest of all," said Raweno. He squashed Owl's head down into his shoulders.

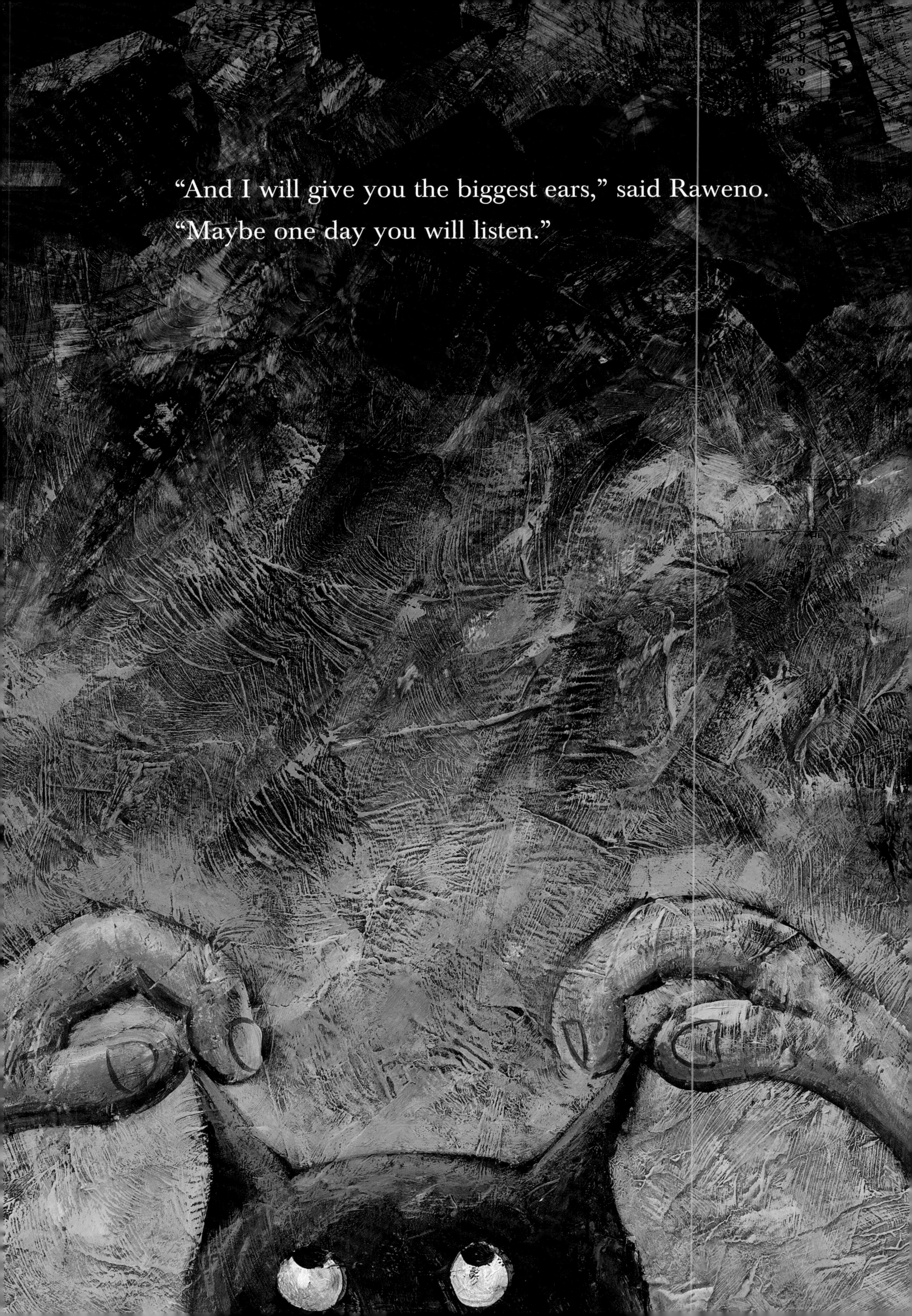

"And I will give you the biggest ears," said Raweno.
"Maybe one day you will listen."

"And your legs for wading along the shore shall be short and fat," said Raweno. "Your scruffy wings and stubby tail will help you sail through branches high in the forest." Raweno rolled owl through the muddy dirt on the ground. "Your fiery feathers shall be the color of the soil."

"And your eyes shall be big," said Raweno. "Too big for the bright sun of the day when I am about. The night shall be your time, hiding all the while in old and broken trees."

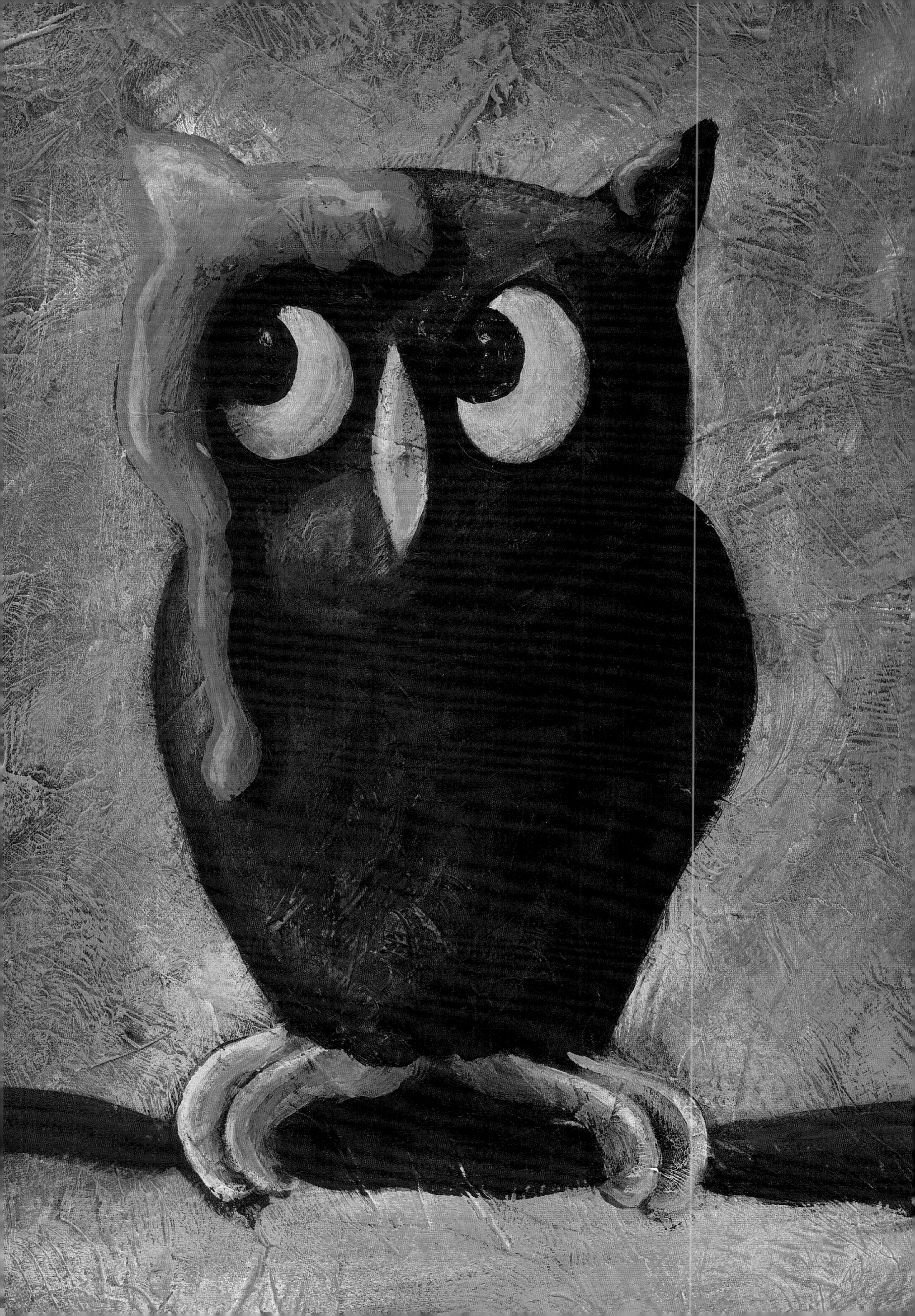

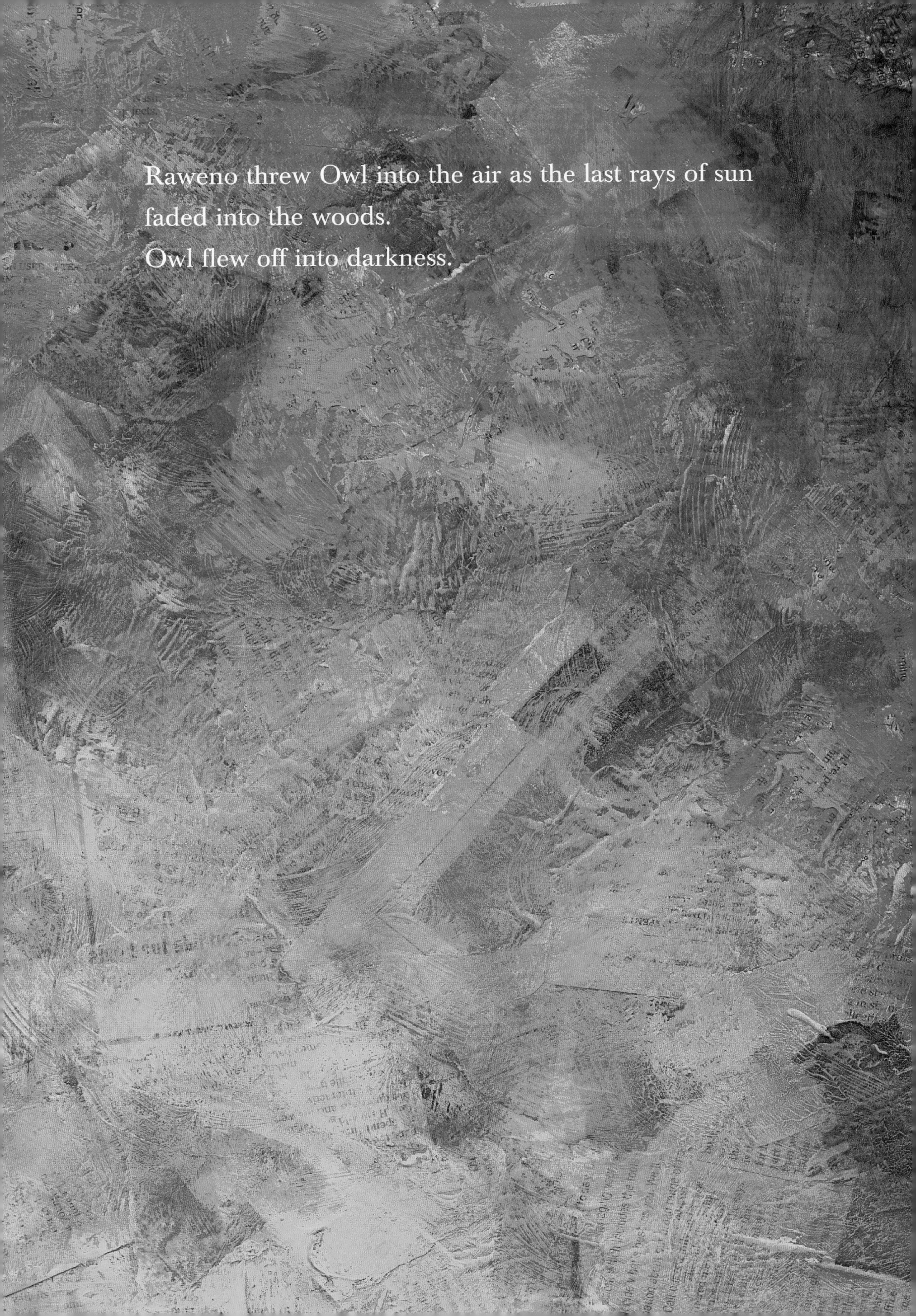

Raweno threw Owl into the air as the last rays of sun faded into the woods.
Owl flew off into darkness.

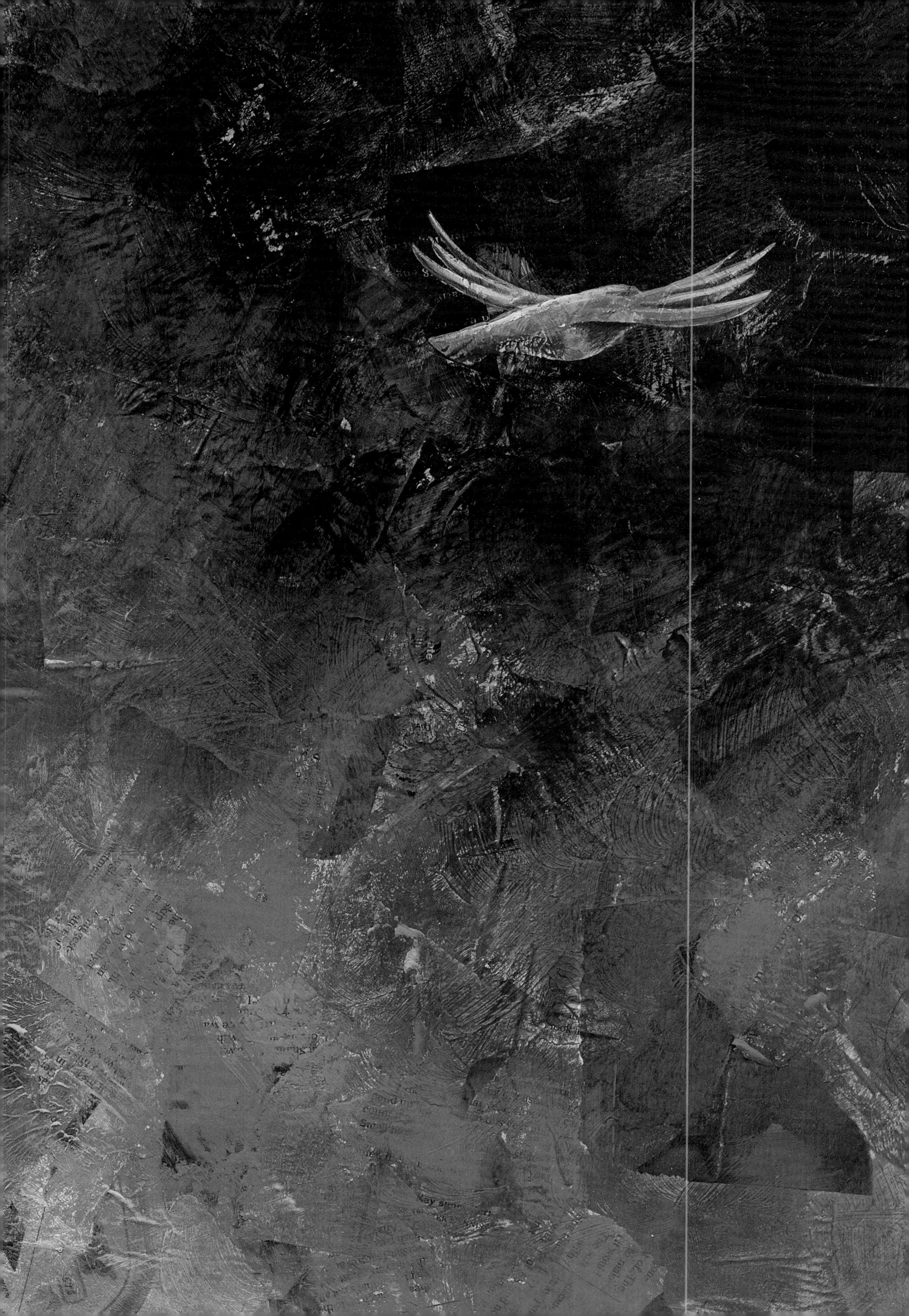

As Raweno lay down to sleep, he wondered where Rabbit, unfinished, had gone.

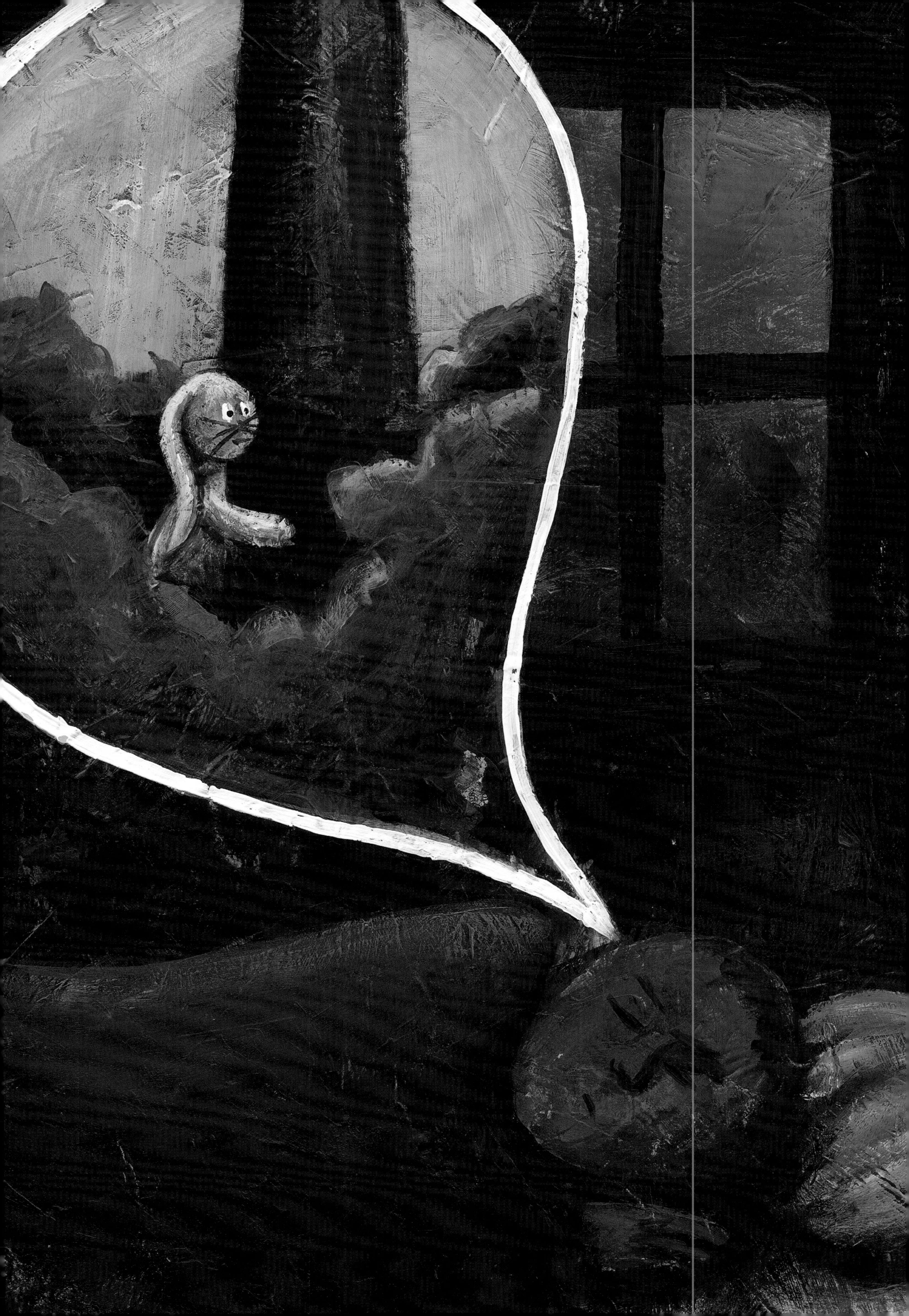

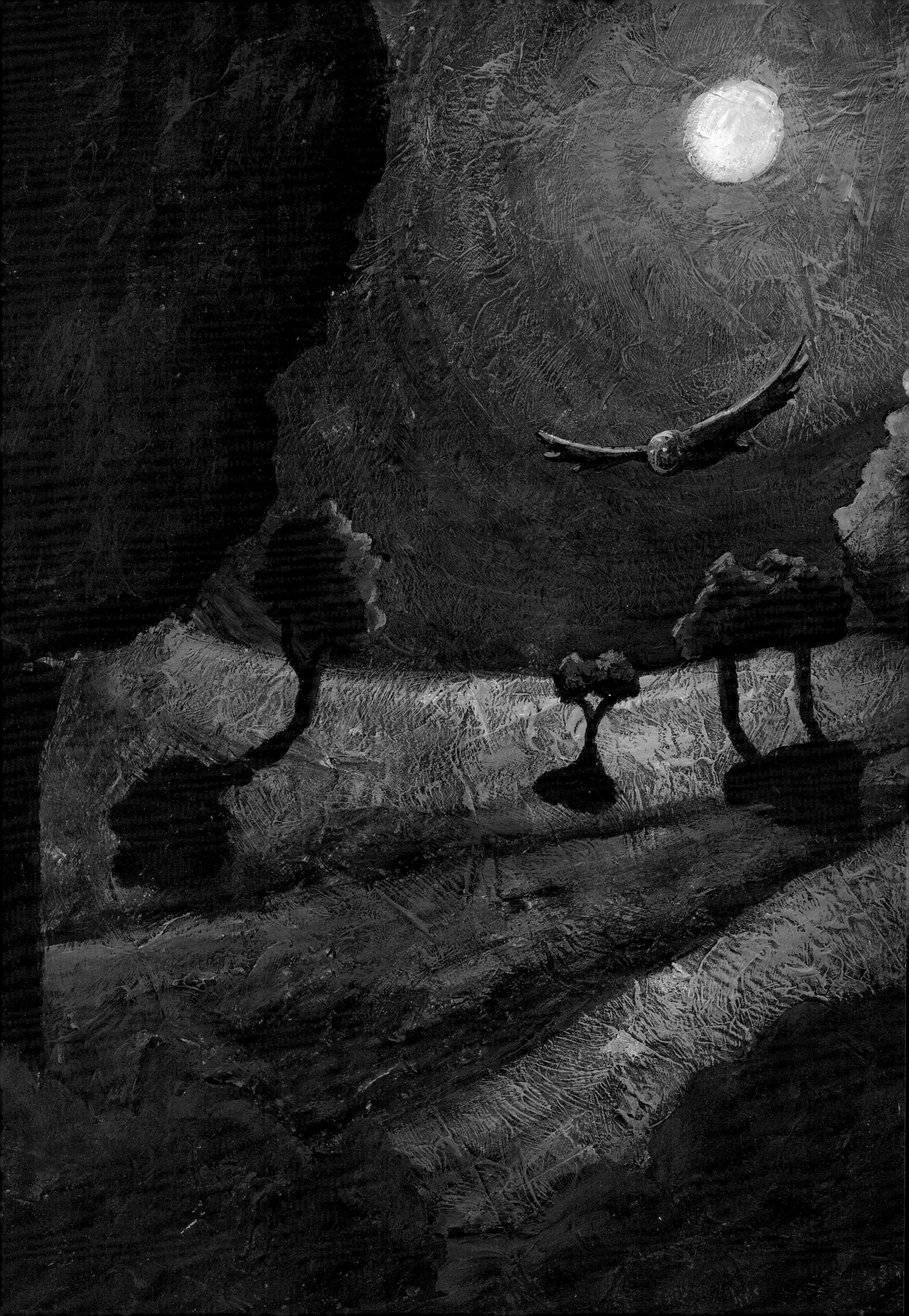